TANGSHAN TIGERS

The Invisible Cloud

D0100874

Dan Lee

PUFFIN

With .... *naw*

PUFFIN BOOKS

Published by the Penguin Group
Penguin Books Ltd, 80 Strand, London WC2R ORL, England
Penguin Group (USA) Inc., 375 Hudson Street, New York, New York 10014, USA
Penguin Group (Canada), 90 Eglinton Avenue East, Suite 700, Toronto, Ontario, Canada M4P 2Y3
(a division of Pearson Penguin Canada Inc.)
Penguin Ireland, 25 St Stephen's Green, Dublin 2, Ireland (a division of Penguin Books Ltd)
Penguin Group (Australia), 250 Camberwell Road, Camberwell, Victoria 3124, Australia
(a division of Pearson Australia Group Pty Ltd)
Penguin Books India Pvt Ltd, 11 Community Centre, Panchsheel Park,
New Delhi – 110 017, India
Penguin Group (NZ), 67 Apollo Drive, Rosedale, North Shore 0632, New Zealand
(a division of Pearson New Zealand Ltd)
Penguin Books (South Africa) (Pty) Ltd, 24 Sturdee Avenue, Rosebank,
Johannesburg 2196, South Africa

Penguin Books Ltd, Registered Offices: 80 Strand, London WC2R ORL, England

puffinbooks.co.uk

Published 2008
1

Series created by Working Partners Ltd, London
Text copyright © Working Partners Ltd, 2008
All rights reserved

The moral right of the author has been asserted

Set in Bembo
Typeset by Palimpsest Book Production Limited, Grangemouth, Stirlingshire
Made and printed in England by Clays Ltd, St Ives plc

British Library Cataloguing in Publication Data
A CIP catalogue record for this book is available from the British Library

ISBN: 978-0-141-32285-8

CONTENTS

A NEW TOURNAMENT

'Matt James!'

'Yes, sir?'

'Those cuts and bruises on your arms – how did you obtain them?'

'Erm . . .' Matt panicked. What was he going to say? Mr Wu, principal of the Beijing International Academy had stopped him at the door to the Assembly Hall. The other students streamed past. Mr Wu, smart as always in a well-cut suit and twinkling black shoes, was staring fixedly through his steel-rimmed spectacles at Matt's left arm. Matt had unthinkingly put on a short-sleeved shirt that morning, and anyone could see the grazes and bruises on his arms. How on earth was he going to explain them?

Matt wondered how Mr Wu would react if he said, *Well, sir, I got them escaping from a cave with the roof coming down on us, underneath the Great Wall of China, after my friends and I had been trapped there by a gang of evil villains.*

It would almost have been worth it, just to see the expression on Mr Wu's face. But he couldn't say this. It would mean exposing the secret of the Tangshan Tigers, the crime-fighting gang that Matt had formed with his friends Olivier, Catarina and Shawn.

'Oh, these cuts and bruises,' he said, playing for time. 'Yes, they are pretty bad, aren't they?'

'So how did you obtain them?' asked Mr Wu.

He needed to come up with a story. But lying didn't come naturally to Matt. He felt tongue-tied. 'How did I obtain them?' he repeated, licking his lips nervously.

'Why don't you just tell Mr Wu the truth, Matt?' said a voice. It was Olivier.

Matt stared at him in confusion. Tell the truth? Did Olivier mean . . . ?

'He's probably embarrassed to admit it, sir,' said Olivier. 'But he's got this super-cool new bike – tungsten-alloy frame, twenty-one gears, the works. He took it out for a spin, and he was going too fast and he jammed the brakes on, and – well, those brakes were a bit too good and he went flying over the handle-bars. That's right, isn't it, Matt?'

'Er, yeah,' Matt said. 'Straight over the handle-bars. It was terrible.'

Mr Wu gave a thin smile. 'You must exercise greater care, Matt,' he said. 'Cycling requires attention and prudence. We do not want one of the stars of our martial arts squad injuring himself, do we?'

'No, sir.'

Mr Wu gave a brief nod and passed into the Assembly Hall. Matt and Olivier followed a little way behind.

'Thanks!' said Matt in a low voice. 'You saved me there. I owe you one.'

Olivier had an amazing knack of coming up with plausible stories under pressure. He was never at a loss for words. And they didn't sound like lies when he told them, more like stories that could and probably should have been true.

'Hey, no problem.'

'I'm gonna wear long-sleeved tops from now on till my arm's healed up,' said Matt. 'I don't want anyone else noticing!'

They went into the hall, threading their

way through the throng of students, and took their places beside Shawn Hung and Catarina Ribeiro.

'Hi, guys!' said Catarina. 'What kept you?'

'Oh, Mr Wu was asking me a few questions about my arm,' said Matt. 'I thought I was going to have to give away – you know what – but Olivier helped me out.'

'Hey, speaking of Mr Wu,' said Catarina, 'do you reckon he'll announce our next tournament today?'

'Hope so,' said Matt. 'If it's all been fixed up.'

'And where do you think it's gonna be?'

'We'll find out,' said Matt. 'Hopefully, it'll mean another adventure!'

Matt looked around him as the Assembly Hall filled up. Even now, after a term at the school, he was still impressed by this place, with its lofty ceiling, imposing stage, high windows, and walls covered in a rich mosaic of lotus flowers, willow trees and Chinese pagodas. The tiles were solar-sensitive, and changed colour throughout the day as the sun rose in the sky. Right now they were a mixture of blues and greens, with a few tints of pink and purple beginning to creep in.

I'm lucky to be here, thought Matt. Lucky to be studying at this amazing Academy. Most of all he was lucky to have such good friends. All four of them were seriously talented martial artists: Matt's speciality was tae kwon-do, Shawn's was judo, Olivier's was kung fu and Catarina's was the Brazilian form of combat, capoeira. They each had some unique skill to bring to the Tangshan Tigers. There was Olivier with his charm and ability to talk his way out of any situation. Shawn with his hi-tech wizardry – he could make any gadget, anything computerized or electronic, do anything he wanted it to. And Catarina was nimble and agile as a circus acrobat. *And me*, he thought. *I've got a photographic memory.*

A hush descended as Mr Wu walked on to the stage. He looked smugly around and cleared his throat. Invisible microphones carried the sound of his voice, amplified but pin-sharp, to every corner of the hall.

'Good morning. It gives me great pleasure to make the following announcement. Our martial arts team – fresh from their triumph over the Shanghai Institute – are to compete in another big tournament. They will be travelling to Japan to compete against the Kyoto Institute of Excellence.'

'Yes!' said Matt, punching the air.

'Oh boy,' said Johnny Goldberg, Matt's friend and room-mate. 'Are you lucky!'

7

Johnny wasn't in the martial arts squad. He was one of the stars of the basketball team.

'Fantastic!' said Matt. 'Japan – I've never been there. I can't wait!'

All eleven members of the squad began chattering excitedly at the prospect. Their coach, Chang Sifu, had told them that another tournament was a possibility. But Chang had said no more than that. He never gave too much away. Now Mr Wu's announcement had made it official.

'I've been to Japan with my dad,' said Olivier. His father was a diplomat and Olivier had travelled a lot. 'You'll like it. It's beautiful – and the food's great.'

'I hope the Kyoto team fight fair, though,' said Shawn. 'Not like the Shanghai team.'

'Me too,' said Matt.

The Shanghai team had used some illegal intimidation tactics against them in the last tournament. 'But, fair or not, we can still beat them. Like we beat Shanghai!'

Mr Wu cleared his throat again and the murmurs of excitement died away. 'I am sure our team, under the excellent tutelage of Chang Sifu, will triumph once again and return with another trophy for my office, er –' he coughed – 'I mean, for the Beijing International Academy.'

Matt was full of excitement about the trip to Kyoto – and so were the other squad members. As they made their way out of the hall at the end of Assembly, it was the only thing anyone could talk about.

'Who do you think's gonna be captain?' asked Shawn. It was Chang Sifu's policy to rotate the captaincy of the squad, giving everyone the chance to lead their team-mates at least once.

'I don't mind,' said Catarina. 'If he offers it

to me, I'll take it. I just want to get out there and compete.'

'He should give it to me,' said Carl Warrick, walking up to join them. 'I'd make the best captain.'

'Oh? Why is that?' enquired Olivier.

''Cause I'm the best!' said Carl.

'Yeah? How come I beat you in the one-on-one in training yesterday then?' demanded Shawn.

'You got lucky, that's all,' said Carl. 'Anyway, that was just training, I wasn't really trying.'

'Yeah, right!'

'There's another reason why I should be captain,' continued Carl. A sly expression stole over his face. Matt felt a stab of anxiety. He thought he saw what Carl was getting at – and he didn't like it.

'What's that?' asked Shawn.

'Put it this way – if I don't make captain, I

might end up saying something I shouldn't. Let something slip out, if you know what I mean.'

'I'm not sure I do,' said Matt quietly, although he was pretty sure he did.

'Oh, I reckon you do,' said Carl with a grin, and walked off to join his friends Miles and Roger.

The Tangshan Tigers looked at each other.

'That's blackmail!' said Shawn, clenching his fists.

Carl had secretly followed them on their last adventure. He did not know everything that had happened, but he knew that they had broken school bounds without permission; he certainly knew enough to make life awkward for them if Mr Wu started asking questions.

'He wouldn't say anything,' said Matt. 'He promised Master Chang –'

'People do break promises sometimes,' said Olivier dryly.

'But what's he trying to say?' said Matt. 'That unless we recommend him for captain —'

'There's no way I'm gonna recommend him!' said Shawn. 'He can say what he likes!'

'Agreed,' said Olivier.

'I'd rather recommend my dog!' said Catarina.

They all laughed.

A burst of Chinese classical music cut across their laughter — the signal that morning class was about to begin. As they hurried down the corridor for maths, Matt said over his shoulder to the others: 'I wouldn't worry about it. Master Chang decides who makes captain — and can you see Carl trying to blackmail Chang?'

The idea of Carl attempting to put pressure on Chang Sifu was ridiculous.

'No way,' said Shawn. 'Does not compute!'

Master Chang had arranged a training session before lunch. That was one of the great things about being in the martial arts squad, thought Matt. You got to cut classes early. At twelve o'clock they assembled in the *kwoon*, or training hall, dressed in their martial arts suits.

Chang stood in the centre, arms by his sides, wearing a plain blue martial arts suit with a black belt. His hair was grey but his face was smooth and unlined. Matt thought that he had never met anyone so physically at ease as Master Chang – he even made standing still look graceful. There was something about the light, loose way he stood that told you he could move with lightning speed if he needed to – but only if he needed to.

'Gather round, please,' he said.

The squad formed a respectful semicircle around him.

'So,' said Chang, 'we are bound for Kyoto.'

Matt and the others whooped with excitement.

Chang held up his hand for silence.

'But I have another important announcement. One member of our squad is shortly to leave us. He is to transfer to another school. By strange coincidence, that school is Kyoto Institute of Excellence. So, assuming he makes the Kyoto squad – and of this I have little doubt – he will be among our opponents in forthcoming tournament.'

A tense hush fell. Matt felt a pang of dismay at the news. He got on so well with all the squad members that he couldn't imagine fighting any of them in a serious competition. Who could it be? Surely not one of the Tangshan Tigers? No way! He looked at them, but they all appeared to be as much in the dark as he was. Shawn frowned, clearly puzzled; Catarina shrugged her shoulders; and Olivier spread his arms as if to say, 'I have no idea.'

Chang did not keep them in suspense much longer.

'The student who is to transfer,' he said, 'is Dani Valerio.'

Matt and everybody else turned to stare at Dani, who grinned sheepishly. Matt didn't know him as well as he knew some of the other squad members, but he liked him a lot. He was Italian, a quiet, serious boy whose speciality was karate.

'Well, Dani,' said Chang. 'I will leave it to you to explain reasons for transfer.'

'I-I will be sorry to leave you guys,' said

Dani. 'My parents are academics, you know, and they both have posts at the University of Kyoto for a year. So I have to go with them. We're leaving tomorrow. They say the Institute at Kyoto is pretty good – but I will be sad to leave Beijing.'

Matt glanced at Chang. His face remained calm, impassive. It was impossible to tell what he was thinking.

There was a pause. Then Matt stepped forward and shook Dani's hand.

'Congratulations,' he said. 'I'm sure you'll get on fine there.'

Other students crowded around to congratulate Dani, slapping him on the back.

'Kyoto's awesome,' said Olivier. 'You'll love it.'

'Don't forget to try the sushi!' said Shawn.

'Best of luck,' said Wolfgang, shaking Dani's hand.

'I bet you'll be captain of the Kyoto team!' said Lola.

'And it's not like we won't see you again,' said Catarina. 'We'll meet you at the tournament.'

'Right,' said Carl. 'And I'm looking forward to kicking your butt, Dani!'

Dani laughed, a bit stiffly. Matt frowned at Carl, unimpressed by his rudeness.

'What are you looking at?' said Carl aggressively.

Chang raised his hand again. 'I would not have put it in quite the way that Carl did. Nevertheless, he has a point. One of you will have to face Dani in the tournament – and, no hard feelings, Dani, but we will do our best to defeat you. There is no avoiding this. And to beat Dani and the rest of Kyoto team – who have reputation as very good fighters, I assure you – we will need complete focus. We must focus like eagles. An eagle, you know, can spot its prey on the ground from a mile high, so keen are its eyes, so intense is its focus. You must focus on your goal like eagle searching for prey. That is what we practise in training session today. Focus.'

'Hey, wait a minute,' protested Carl. He pointed at Dani. 'I won't train with a traitor!'

'He's not a traitor!' said Matt.

'But he's gonna be fighting against us – he should be up in his room packing his bags, not getting a few last training tips!'

Dani looked uncomfortable, Matt saw. He was shuffling his feet and a blush spread over his cheeks.

'Dani is a member of the Beijing Academy, and of this squad, until tomorrow,' said Master Chang. 'I would never deprive anyone of opportunity to learn martial arts. Dani is welcome in this *kwoon* until he departs. Now, if there are no more questions –'

'Yeah, well I do have another question!' said Carl rudely. 'What about the captain? Who's it gonna be?'

'If you would simply listen, Carl,' said Chang with a touch of sharpness – enough to make Carl flush and look down at his toes – 'you would find out sooner. Today I set a task: to maintain complete focus in conditions of extreme distraction. Whoever performs best in this task will earn right to captain his – or her – team-mates.'

Matt saw that Carl looked a little bit less confident now. Matt felt a tingle of excited anticipation at the task that lay ahead. *Focus*, he told himself. *That's all you've got to do: keep focused*. But he couldn't stop one niggling doubt worming its way into his brain. What did Chang mean by 'extreme distraction'?

Chapter 2

SNAKES IN THE DARK!

Matt and the others waited to hear Chang Sifu announce the task.

'Task is to perform basic *kata* —'

'Oh, is that all!' said Carl loudly, and Matt could hear the relief in his voice. 'No problem: I've been doing *kata* since —'

'I've been doing *kata* since before I was born!' said Olivier, in his perfect imitation of Carl's Australian accent. 'I was doing them in my mummy's tummy. It's true, you know — it showed up on the ultrasound scan!'

There was a burst of laughter. Carl glared at Olivier. Chang cut off the laughter with a slight motion of his hand.

'Task is to perform basic *kata*,' he continued, 'without any break in rhythm no matter what distractions may ensue.'

Matt watched carefully, memorizing every detail, as Chang demonstrated the *kata*. It was a simple enough sequence of moves: two steps forward, a block, a high kick, a spear-hand thrust, two steps back.

'Find own space and begin,' said Chang quietly.

Matt began the *kata*, not looking at anyone else, concentrating on his own movements, trying his best to mimic the easy grace and powerful rhythm that Chang had shown them. He soon fell into the swing of it, moving easily, naturally. The only sounds in the *kwoon* were the thud of bare feet on the mat and the students' heavy breathing as the exertion took its toll. There were no distractions as yet.

Out of the corner of his eye Matt saw Chang slip away somewhere, and had to force himself not to turn his head. He returned his concentration to his own movements: step, step, block, kick, thrust . . .

Then he heard a muffled *thud* as the electric power was shut down, and all the lights went out.

The *kwoon* was plunged into near-darkness. Matt sensed two of the students near him hesitate and break step; one of them gave a nervous giggle.

'Two students who paused, please to step out of formation,' came Chang's voice. 'Others continue.'

Matt kept going. His eyes became accustomed to the gloom; he saw the pale forms of the other squad members moving beside him, and the dark figure of Chang standing over by the door.

A moment later he saw Chang slip through the door, which clicked shut after him.

Where had he gone? The uncertainty almost caused Matt to falter – but he kept moving, step, step, block, kick, thrust . . . Chang might reappear any minute, or in ten minutes, and the important thing was to make sure that when he did Matt was still keeping the rhythm going. He was aware of the Tangshan Tigers beside him, moving steadily – but he kept his focus firmly on his own movement.

The door opened again and Chang re-entered. He carried what appeared to be a sack over his shoulder. He walked slowly to the edge of the mat and upended the sack.

A mass of writing black shapes tumbled out. Long, sinuous shapes that quickly separated and began to swarm across the mat . . .

Snakes!

Matt felt a severe jolt inside and sweat sprang out on the palms of his hands. He didn't have a phobia about snakes, but he didn't exactly like them either. They gave him a sort of shivery feeling.

There was pandemonium. Several students screamed and Lola, the Nigerian girl, forgot about the *kata* altogether and sprinted off the mat to take cover in the changing rooms.

Matt somehow kept his body going through the motions. Surely even Chang, unpredictable though his methods were, would not introduce venomous snakes into a training session! They had to be harmless – grass snakes, probably.

'All students who broke rhythm leave

formation,' came Chang's voice again.
'Remaining five students continue.'

Matt saw that the other students who had
held their nerve were Catarina, Shawn,
Olivier – and Carl. You had to hand it to
Carl, thought Matt. Carl was frightened of
the dark, he knew, and to cope with that
plus snakes must take an awesome amount of
willpower. He must really want the captaincy.
Well, so do I, thought Matt, trying to lose
himself again in the rhythm of the *kata*.

But it was difficult to maintain focus
knowing the snakes were on the loose, seeing
them slither nearer and nearer. Matt noticed
one in particular that seemed to be coming
straight for him: its body weaved from side
to side in s-shaped curves, and its blunt head
seemed to be seeking him out.

He heard an earsplitting screech. A snake
had slithered across Carl's bare toes and made

him hop from foot to foot in a desperate
effort to shake it off. Matt burst out laughing.
He just couldn't help it.

'Carl, Matt – both leave formation, please.'

Matt went and stood by the wall. He
didn't feel too bad about failing the task.
OK, so he wouldn't be captain now, but at
least it would still go to one of the
Tangshan Tigers.

He didn't have to wait long to find out
who. Shawn and Olivier were both freaked
out by a snake coiling over the mat towards
them. It was easy to see why. The snake's
forked tongue flickered in and out of its
mouth as it peered up at the boys' faces.

'Hey, that was one mean-looking snake,'
Matt muttered to Shawn as he stepped off
the mat.

'No kidding!' agreed Shawn.

Catarina was the only one left, still

gracefully performing the *kata*, neatly stepping over the snakes writhing around her.

Chang switched the lights back on. He began gently, carefully, collecting the snakes and putting them back in the sack.

'This place is a madhouse!' burst out Carl. 'We could have been bitten – poisoned!'

'I do not think so,' said Chang mildly, holding one of the snakes and stroking its head. Now that the lights were on, Matt could see the creature's bright green skin, marked with a diamond pattern. 'These are harmless grass snakes. Beautiful creatures. Well, the task is over. Catarina, you will captain the Beijing International Academy Martial Arts Squad in our trip to Kyoto.'

Matt ran across to Catarina and clapped her on the shoulder. 'Hey, well done! That was fantastic!'

The other Tangshan Tigers gathered round to congratulate her.

'Go, Catarina!'

'Captain Catarina!'

'Weren't you scared?'

Catarina grinned. 'A few little snakes? What's to be scared of?'

Carl snorted loudly. 'It's just ridiculous! I can't believe we're gonna be captained by a –'

Catarina swivelled round to face him, her eyes flashing. 'Yes? By a – a what?'

They glared at each other. Then Carl shook his head and stormed out of the *kwoon*. Matt and his friends laughed.

'Let's go get changed and have some lunch,' said Shawn.

'I wonder what's on the menu today?' said Olivier.

'Snake and kidney pie!' said Matt, and they

all laughed again as they ran to the changing rooms.

Ten days later, Matt, his team-mates, Master Chang and Mr Figgis (their history teacher who was coming along as the second teacher in charge) were in a sleek, air-conditioned coach, pulling up at a private airport to the east of Beijing, surrounded by green fields. The airport, though small, was ultra-modern, with a slender steel control tower that looked like something out of a science-fiction movie.

Matt felt his excitement growing. He couldn't wait to be airborne and on his way to Japan. He nudged Olivier, who was sitting next to him. Olivier put down the book he was reading – *A History of Kyoto*.

'Yeah?'

'Look – we're here – that must be our plane!'

Standing on the runway was a private chartered jet, its wings gleaming in the sunlight. It was sleek, shiny, with a conical nosepiece – much smaller than a standard passenger aeroplane.

'Cool!' said Shawn's voice from behind him. 'That's a Learjet XL5 – state of the art, the latest design. They cruise at a thousand miles an hour!'

They all piled off the coach. Chang Sifu shepherded them along a path and into the airport building. It was quiet and compact, completely unlike big international airports Matt had been to. And it was much, much quicker to pass through. There was no queue to check their luggage – a quick glance at their passports by a uniformed official, and then they were following Chang and Mr Figgis through a doorway and out on to the sunlit tarmac again. The Learjet XL5 stood waiting to receive them.

The interior of the jet was much smaller than a commercial airliner, but there were far fewer seats, and they had them all to themselves, so it felt much more spacious. The cabin was luxurious, with a deep carpet on the floor and leather seats. It was more like being in a flying hotel than on a plane, Matt thought. Not that you could forget you were on a plane: there was a panel on the seat in front of him that showed a 3D computerized image of the jet flying across Asia, over the East China Sea to Japan, and you could zoom in and out to see just the terrain directly below or the bigger picture of the whole continent. The panel also gave the altitude and cruising speed. Matt couldn't stop watching it.

The flight passed quickly, what with bantering and laughing and chatting with the other squad members, and playing with Shawn's new games console, which had a brand-new high-definition martial arts game on it, and eating the delicious food – sushi in a little plastic box. Plus there was the view out of the window – the land mass of South Korea glimpsed through the clouds, then the deep blue water of the Sea of Japan.

'What do you reckon?' said Shawn. 'You feel ready for the tournament?'

'I think so,' said Matt. 'Yeah, I feel OK.' He was feeling on top form, but he didn't want to say too much about that; it might be tempting fate.

It was mid-afternoon when the plane descended at Kyoto Airport. Matt stretched and breathed deeply, glad to be out in the open air again after hours in a pressurized cabin. It was a fine spring day and the air felt cool and fresh.

In the arrivals hall, Chang led them straight through to passport control.

'What about our bags, sir?' asked Shawn.

'They will be sent on to Kyoto Institute. They will be waiting for us when we arrive there – but first I want to take you somewhere in the city.'

'Where's that, sir?' asked Matt.

'To a temple,' replied Chang. 'Toji Temple – famous Eastern Temple of Kyoto.'

Outside, another sleek silver coach was waiting for them. As it nosed its way through the city, Matt looked out of the window. This was his first time in Kyoto. It was like taking a trip back in time. Obviously Kyoto was less busy than Beijing, but it wasn't just that – the whole place seemed built on a smaller, more delicate scale. There didn't seem to be any skyscrapers at all.

Matt pointed this out to Olivier, who said: 'Sure – didn't you know, there was a law passed here to say no buildings higher than three storeys could be built. That's because there are so many historic buildings here, temples and stuff – they didn't want them to get hidden away.'

Matt saw this in every street they passed. Buddhist temples were frequent, with sloping roofs and verandas, often painted bright red or gleaming gold, beautiful in the spring sunlight. And even the ordinary buildings, the houses and offices, looked old and picturesque, painted white, cream and pink.

'This is gorgeous,' said Catarina. 'It's like – a picture!'

'Fantastic!' said Matt.

'I told you you'd like it here,' said Olivier.

The only person who didn't seem impressed by the scenery was Carl Warrick.

'Why do we have to go see this old temple anyway?' he complained from the back of the coach. 'What's the point? Why can't we just go to the Institute and chill? We've been travelling all day – and the tournament's tomorrow; we need to rest!'

Chang turned round in his seat to answer him. 'You will find this helpful, Carl. The excitement of travel, of being in a foreign city, all this may prevent you from focusing on your task. Trip to temple will help you feel calm. We will do relaxation exercise there.'

'Oh great,' groaned Carl. 'What is it this time, sitting with a frog on our heads, or –'

'Besides,' said Chang, taking no notice of Carl's rudeness, 'you do not come to Kyoto every day – do you not want to see something of it?'

'It's a historic city,' said Mr Figgis, the history teacher. 'The ancient capital of Japan. You should make the most of your visit here.'

'Yeah, right,' muttered Carl.

The coach was turning through a gate into the grounds of the Eastern Temple.

'Come on, you guys!' said Matt. He was so eager to look around he was the first off the coach.

What immediately struck him was how busy it was – the square in front of the temple was filled with stalls selling clothes, shoes, bags, hats, garments and accessories of all kinds, and there were hundreds of shoppers milling around.

'I didn't expect anything like this,' he said to Mr Figgis, who was standing close by. 'What is this, a market?'

'It is the Kobi-san flea market, held in these temple grounds on the twenty-first of every month,' explained Mr Figgis. 'An ancient tradition.'

They walked through the busy, bustling market. Catarina kept wanting to stop to look at the shoes on sale but Chang gently but firmly kept everyone moving.

'Oh, but look at these sandals!' she said. 'Can't I just –'

'I will show you something more interesting than shoes,' Chang said. 'Follow, please.'

Once they were through the market, the temple appeared. Matt caught his breath.

The Eastern Temple was larger than anything they had seen in Beijing: a massive wooden structure, a sloping ornamented roof with beams picked out in gold that shone in the sunshine. In front of the temple was a still green lake, so smooth that the temple building was reflected in it as a perfect, upside-down copy. All around the temple were cherry trees in blossom – thick, glowing pink and white. Petals floated gently down from the boughs as they passed underneath, and covered the path leading around the lake towards the temple. The scent of the blossom was everywhere – rich, sweet, perfumed.

Matt had never seen or smelt or imagined anything so beautiful. He heard Catarina say softly: 'Wow . . . Look at that!'

Even Carl appeared to be mesmerized.

'What do you think, Carl?' Matt asked him. 'Glad we came?'

Carl shrugged. 'It's just a big wooden house and some pink flowers,' he said.

Funny how Carl is, thought Matt. Surely it would have been easier just to say, 'Yes, it's beautiful.' But that would have meant saying something positive rather than something negative – and Carl didn't seem to like doing that.

Two Buddhist monks were waiting for them at the steps of the temple. They wore orange robes and their heads were shaved. They had deep, dark, thoughtful eyes. They bowed at Master Chang's approach.

Chang bowed in return. He said something to them in a foreign language – *He speaks Japanese!* thought Matt – and they replied.

Chang turned to his students. 'We will go into temple now. Please remove shoes and place on shelves. We are going to see special garden.'

They followed Chang up the steps, which ended in a veranda that ran all the way round the temple building. There were wooden shelves along the wall where they left their shoes. Then they went through the door and inside the temple.

It was dim and cool inside. The ceiling was high. At the far end Matt saw a huge marble statue of the Buddha, sitting calm and serene. They passed by this and out through another door – and into the strangest garden Matt had ever seen.

It was rectangular, about the size of a tennis court. It was covered in fine white sand, absolutely smooth and flat. Dotted around it were five large black rocks – not placed symmetrically, but spaced so that no one rock was too close to any of the others. There were no plants or flowers, no living things at all except for some greenish moss that grew on the sides of the boulders. Wooden decking ran round the garden so that you could view it without treading on the sand.

Matt's first impression was that this was a pretty unusual garden, with no flowers or trees. But there was something oddly impressive about it. The simplicity, the stillness, the quietness. The bustle of the flea market seemed a million miles away.

'But – this is a funny sort of garden,' said Lola, sounding puzzled. 'Where are the flowers? Where is the grass?'

'This garden is over four hundred years old,' said Chang softly. 'A perfect example of Zen garden-maker's art. Say nothing, but focus on garden and meditate. To meditate, all you need to do is empty head of thoughts. Every time a thought comes, return focus to garden. Become one with this place.'

Silence fell. Matt gazed at the garden, allowing the stillness to enter his soul. How strange to think that these rocks had been here, unchanged, for four hundred summers and four hundred winters.

He felt his breathing slow down. He let his

gaze wander from one rock to the next, to the white sand in between, emptying his mind of thoughts.

How much time passed he had no idea. Twenty minutes, half an hour? But when Chang finally moved and spoke, saying it was time to go to the Institute, he felt completely rested and refreshed.

'I feel like a new person,' said Matt to the other Tigers.

'I know what you mean,' said Olivier. 'Peaceful.'

'All cleaned out inside,' said Catarina.

'Chang certainly knows what he's doing,' said Shawn as they walked back under the cherry trees to where the coach was parked. 'We needed that.'

'It even worked for Carl,' said Matt, pointing at Carl, who was walking by himself, not talking, his face thoughtful.

'Yeah,' said Catarina. 'But I wonder how long that will last!'

Like the Beijing International Academy, the Kyoto Institute of Excellence was a large, modern hi-tech building in its own grounds. The school building was surrounded by avenues of cherry trees in full blossom. It had a high glass atrium with a tree growing up to the top floor and a moving pavement to take you from one end to the other. There were portraits in coloured glass of samurai warriors around the walls.

'Hey, this is pretty cool!' said Catarina.

'Almost as good as the Beijing Academy,' said Olivier.

'But not quite!' laughed Matt.

Their luggage was waiting for them behind the reception desk. A polite, smiling young female receptionist made sure that everyone was reunited with their cases, and showed them up to their dormitories, which were on the fifth floor. Chang accompanied them as far as the landing.

'Unpack, then relax,' he told them. 'Tonight is free night! Enjoy yourselves.'

Matt was sharing a dorm with Shawn and Olivier. They went in and unpacked. The room was light and airy, with futons for beds – slatted wooden platforms with a thin white mattress rolled up at the end. Matt unrolled his and sat on it. It was firm, but comfortable.

'Hey, I like these beds,' he said.

'Yeah, futons,' said Shawn. 'Great, aren't they? It'll be fun to sleep so close to the ground – you can just roll out of bed in the morning!'

'But what do we do now?' asked Olivier. 'We can't sit on our futons all evening.'

There was a tap at the door. Matt rose and opened it.

Standing there were four boys and two girls of about their age. They were all dressed in blue and red tracksuits, with Japanese characters down the sides of the legs. Dani was with them. He stood slightly to one side, a half-smile on his face.

Matt tensed slightly. He remembered how arrogant and hostile the Shanghai team had been at the last tournament – were the Kyoto fighters up to the same tricks? Had they come to try to psyche out the Beijing team?

The boy at the head of the group, a tall and athletic figure, took a step forward and held out his hand.

'Hi, I'm Miguel,' he said with a friendly smile. 'I'm captain of the Kyoto team. We came to welcome you.'

'Oh – thanks,' said Matt. 'It's good to be here. I'm Matt. Our captain's not here, she's in another dorm.'

'Well, how about we all meet up and get to know each other?' said Miguel. 'There's a common room on this landing – see you there in a few minutes?'

'Sure,' said Matt. 'We'd like that.'

The Kyoto team left, but Dani remained behind for a moment.

'It's good to see you guys again.'

He came in and sat down on a futon.

'Good to see you too,' said Matt. 'How are you getting on here?'

'What are the Kyoto students like?' asked Olivier.

'I've made some friends already,' said Dani. 'They're great guys – especially the martial arts team.'

'Oh, that's good,' said Matt. He couldn't

help feeling slightly hurt that Dani seemed
to have forgotten his Beijing team-mates
so quickly. Then Dani added: 'They're
nearly as great as the Beijing Academy
team!'

Matt and the others laughed.

Ten minutes later, they all met in the
Common Room. Catarina, as team captain,
introduced the squad. She found some little
bit of information to add to each person's
name – 'This is Matt, he's a tae kwon-do
expert – oh, and he also never forgets
anything, so you be careful what you say
around him! This is Olivier, he does ju-jitsu
and speaks three languages. Here's Shawn,
judo expert and techno-wizard.' She even
found something nice to say about Carl –
'He's a *karateka*, and his dad's a famous karate
champion.'

She put everyone at their ease. *She's born to be team captain*, Matt thought.

Miguel introduced the Kyoto team in the same way. When he came to Dani, Catarina smiled and said, 'Don't worry, we know about him! Italian, specializes in karate, parents are academics at the university here, likes skateboarding. Right, Dani?'

'Right,' said Dani, laughing.

'Who was your last tournament against?' asked Matt.

One of the Kyoto team, a Canadian boy named Neil answered. 'Tokyo Central High School. And we beat them!'

So both teams were coming into the contest on the back of a victory, thought Matt. 'We won our last tournament too,' he said. 'So this should be a good one!'

'I'm sure it will be,' said Miguel. 'And may the best team win!'

He said it in such a sporting way that Matt began to feel sure they wouldn't be trying any dirty tricks.

'Well, look, you guys,' continued Miguel. 'We've got the evening to ourselves – our teachers are having a meet and greet thing downstairs in the Assembly Hall. Why don't we have our own meet and greet? We can eat together in the refectory and then go to the Games Room, play some video games, some table tennis, shoot some pool – what do you say?'

Catarina glanced round at her team-mates. Matt nodded at her.

'Sure!' she said. 'Why not?'

'OK then – see you down in the refectory.'

The Kyoto team left. 'Well, they seem like pretty nice people, no?' said Catarina.

Most of the squad nodded agreement.

49

Except Carl. 'You guys are so naive! Can't you see it's all an act?'

'What do you mean, an act?' demanded Matt.

'They're just trying to soften us up! I don't trust them. We shouldn't be playing games with them – we're here for a martial arts contest, or have you forgotten?'

'They've asked us to socialize with them and as team captain I'm saying we accept,' said Catarina. 'What do the rest of you think?'

'I think,' said Matt, 'that we should go and have a good time!'

They all shared a big table together in the refectory.

'This food's delicious,' said Olivier. He was eating a traditional Japanese dish of chicken *sukiyaki* with rice.

'Olivier loves his food,' commented Catarina.

'Well, who doesn't?' said Miguel. 'Hey, Dani was telling us about your coach – he sounds like quite a guy.'

'He is,' said Matt. He told the Kyoto team the story of the snakes, and how Catarina came to be team captain. They all laughed.

Matt got the strange sensation that he was being stared at. He looked round and saw a boy standing near another table glaring across at them. The boy was tall, with cropped blond hair, and his eyes seemed to burn like lasers. Matt looked away again and was about to ask Miguel who the boy was, but Neil was talking.

'That's amazing!' said Neil. 'Sensei Simon wouldn't do anything like that. He's good, really knows his stuff – but he's pretty straight-ahead and no-nonsense in his training.'

'Who is he?' asked Shawn.

'Our coach. That's him over there at the teacher's table,' said Dani. 'Talking to Chang.'

Chang and Sensei Simon were deep in conversation. Matt saw Sensei Simon point at the blond boy who had glared at them and say something to Chang; Chang nodded and regarded the boy thoughtfully. The boy was still casting glances of hatred across at the table where the martial arts teams sat – but nobody except Matt seemed to notice. Obviously a kid with a problem. Matt decided to ignore him.

'How about we go to the Games Room then?' said Miguel, when they had all finished.

'Sure thing!' said Catarina.

Matt enjoyed the meet and greet in the Games Room. The only person who didn't join in was Carl. He just played video games all on his own, shouting 'Yes!' or 'Gotcha!' whenever he blew something up on the screen. But everybody else hung out together.

They played a mini-pool tournament, which the Beijing team won by six games to five. Matt was a bit of an ace at pool and he took the last frame against Miguel, potting a long black with a satisfying *crack*. Then they played a mini-table-tennis tournament, and this time Kyoto won.

'That makes it one-all then,' said Miguel. 'What shall we do for a decider?'

Catarina looked at her watch and said regretfully: 'It's nearly ten o'clock, you guys. Chang said we should be back in the dorm by ten. Got a big day tomorrow!'

'I guess the martial arts tournament will be the decider,' said Shawn.

'Reckon so,' said Martina, one of the Kyoto team.

'Sure,' said Miguel. 'We'd better get our eight hours too. Well, it's been fun.'

'Thanks for asking us,' said Matt. 'Goodnight, Miguel – goodnight, you guys. See you all tomorrow.'

They took the high-speed lifts up to the dormitory floor. The Kyoto team disappeared in the direction of their dorms. Matt and his room-mates were about to do the same when Catarina said: 'Hold on, I just remembered – Chang said he would come up to see us before we went to bed; check we settled in and stuff. We'd better hang here for a while.'

There was a communal seating area that linked the dorms, with low comfortable chairs. They settled down to wait, yawning.

They didn't have to wait long. The door

opened and Chang Sifu came into the room.

Matt and the rest of the squad rose to their feet and gave Chang the traditional Chinese sign of respect, holding both hands before their chests in greeting – this was something they often did when Master Chang entered a room.

Usually, Chang responded by offering his own hands in return. This time, that didn't happen. Chang stared straight ahead and started to walk past them, stumbling slightly as he headed for his room at the end of the passage.

Matt and his friends exchanged puzzled glances. It was bizarre. To ignore them completely like this would have been rude by anyone's standards – but for the courteous and dignified Chang Sifu it was off the scale.

It was clear that Chang wasn't himself. Looking more closely, Matt saw that his eyes were wide and staring, and he walked with a slow, unsteady tread.

'Sifu?' said Matt. 'Are you all right?'

Chang came to a stop and stared at Matt. 'I am all right,' he said in a dazed voice.

'Did you – did you have a good time at the meet and greet?'

'The meet and greet,' repeated Chang slowly. 'Yes, I had good time at the meet and greet.' He put his hand to his forehead. His eyes were almost closed.

'Is something wrong, sir?'

'Something wrong, something wrong,' muttered Chang, as though unable to make sense of the words.

Carl planted himself in front of Master Chang. 'Yeah, is there anything wrong with you?' he said loudly and slowly, as if speaking to an infant. 'You look like there is something wrong with you!'

Matt couldn't believe Carl's rudeness. Catarina took Carl's arm and pulled him to one side.

'Leave it, Carl,' she said. 'You don't have to speak to him like that!'

Chang didn't seem to notice. 'I wish you all good luck for tomorrow,' he said in a sleepy voice, resuming his slow walk up the passage and disappearing into his room.

A faint but unmistakable scent lingered behind him.

'What's that smell?' said Wolfgang.

'Dunno,' said Shawn. 'Flowers?'

Matt felt troubled. He was so used to seeing Chang master of himself, so used to admiring him for his self-possession and composure that it was disturbing to see him acting strangely. There was an uneasy silence.

'Do you think he's ill?' asked Lola.

Carl laughed harshly. 'You guys really are

57

naive! Isn't it obvious what's wrong with him?'

'No,' said Catarina. 'Maybe you'd better tell us.'

'He's come from a party, hasn't he? He's overdone it – it's totally obvious!'

'I don't believe that,' said Catarina.

'Nor do I,' said Shawn.

The pleasant atmosphere of earlier in the evening was spoilt now. The squad drifted off to bed, not saying much, looking worried.

Matt lay down on his futon and tried to sleep, but sleep wouldn't come. What if Chang was really ill? Should they have called a doctor? He shifted around to find a comfortable position to fall asleep in, but couldn't. Shawn and Olivier were soon asleep, to judge by their steady breathing, but Matt couldn't settle.

He got up and went to look out of the

open window, gazing at the dark rustling trees outside. The scent of cherry blossom wafted in through the window.

Of course Chang hadn't drunk too much, Matt thought suddenly. It was impossible. It simply wasn't in his character. But he'd smelt of something. He'd smelt of . . . cherry blossom. But why? Chang had not been outside that evening, as far as Matt knew. He'd been in the school, first in the refectory and then in the Assembly Hall for the teachers' meet and greet. Not wandering around beneath cherry trees.

'You'd better get some sleep, Matt,' Olivier called gently from the other side of the room. 'Big day tomorrow!'

'Yeah – you're right,' said Matt. He got back under the sheets of the futon. He was in a strange bed, in a strange school, in a strange country. And tomorrow he had to help win a tournament for his Academy. He turned and gazed at the rustling cherry trees, silhouetted against a full moon. *I've got to do the best I can tomorrow*, he thought to himself. He hoped Chang Sifu would be back on form in the morning. Matt wasn't sure he could do himself justice without his teacher.

Chapter 3

STRANGE SCENTS

Matt's head felt heavy. Not exactly a full-on headache, but a sort of dull discomfort whenever he moved his head. He'd had bad dreams in the night and they'd left behind a creeping feeling. Normally Matt felt wide awake in the morning, but today he would gladly have crawled back into bed.

There was an excited atmosphere in the refectory. Everyone was geared up for the tournament. Matt heard students talking about it as they went by, pointing out the Beijing team.

'There they are!'

'That tall girl's the captain.'

'What do you think – will we beat them?'

'We'd better – we beat Tokyo!'

Their comments made Matt feel deflated. He'd never felt less like fighting in a martial arts tournament.

'You all right, Matt?' asked Olivier, who was sitting opposite him at the breakfast table in the refectory.

'Not great,' admitted Matt. 'I woke up feeling pretty groggy. Like I'm still half asleep.'

'Me too,' said Shawn. There were dark circles under his eyes.

'Yeah, and me,' said Catarina. Her usually bright alert face was puffy and tired. 'I don't feel a hundred per cent today, I gotta say.'

'What's got into you lot?' said Olivier.

'You'd better shape up – we've got a tournament to win! Try some of this Japanese food – it's really good.' He shovelled rice and fermented soya beans into his mouth.

'I guess you're right,' said Matt. He helped himself to some food. But he didn't have much of an appetite. He poured himself a glass of green tea. That was better – bitter and refreshing.

He was pouring himself a second glass when Chang Sifu entered the refectory. Matt saw that he wasn't in much better shape than last night. His eyes still had that glazed look and he walked slowly and hesitantly. He was with the Kyoto team's coach, Sensei Simon, and Simon had the same glazed look.

A crash from the other side of the hall made Matt turn his head. Mr Figgis, the history teacher, had dropped his tray. He bent slowly, clumsily, to pick it up. Another teacher walked across the hall, yawning, his hand held to his head.

What on earth was going on?

'Listen,' said Matt in a low voice. The others bent across the table towards him. 'Something weird is happening here.'

'Yeah, I thought that too,' said Shawn. 'Everyone looks like they're sleepwalking!'

'We need to have a meeting,' said Matt. 'Let's go back to the dorm.'

'We'd better let Chang know we're going,' said Catarina. 'Just in case he wonders where we are – he won't want us going missing the morning of the tournament.'

They walked over to Chang's table. Chang was sitting staring absently at a glass of fruit juice.

'Sifu?' said Catarina. 'We've finished our breakfast – is it all right if we go back to the dorms?'

Chang turned and eyed them. He gave a weird slow-motion smile. 'Of course,' he said. 'Just remember – broken sword makes poor walking-stick.'

'Sorry?' said Catarina. 'I don't –'

'Broken sword makes poor walking-stick,' repeated Chang. 'You understand.'

Matt looked at the others. He had no idea what their teacher was talking about. None of them knew what to say.

The high-speed lifts whisked them up to the dorms. They were glass-walled, so you could see the floors of the school dropping away as you ascended.

Up in the dorm, they each sat on a futon. 'There's something wrong with Chang, that's clear,' Matt said. 'He looks odd, and that stuff about the broken sword and the walking-stick –'

'You're right,' said Olivier. 'Master Chang often says things that you have to think about before you get them — but that made no sense at all!'

'He must be ill,' said Catarina.

'But it's not just him!' said Matt. 'Did you see how Mr Figgis looked? And the Kyoto coach? And I spotted a few other teachers who didn't look right.'

'And it's not just the teachers!' said Shawn. 'I don't feel good, and nor do you, Matt, nor Catarina.'

'I feel OK, for some reason,' said Olivier. 'But I take your point. There's something strange happening.'

'But what could it be?' said Catarina. 'Some sort of virus?'

'A virus that smells of cherry blossom?' said Matt. He glanced out of the window at the cherry trees.

'Why do you say that?' asked Olivier.

'Last night, when Chang came in, did anyone notice the scent that seemed to follow him?'

Catarina snapped her fingers. 'Yes! I was wondering what that smell was. Cherry blossom, that's right!'

'I don't like the sound of that,' said Shawn slowly. 'I was reading something recently in an online science article. It was about a chemical that smells like something. It might have been cherry blossom, I can't remember.'

'Can you find it again?'

'Sure.'

Shawn went to his backpack and pulled out his laptop. He flicked it open, clicked to establish a wi-fi connection and searched for the *Science Today* website. The other Tangshan Tigers crowded round as he scrolled down through the pages.

'Here it is!' said Shawn, jabbing his finger at an article about the use of ethylene as an anaesthetic. 'That's it! Oh, but wait. It says it has a sweet smell, but it doesn't say anything about cherry blossom.'

He tossed the laptop on the bed.

'Back to square one,' said Olivier.

Matt picked up the laptop and scanned the article. ' "The symptoms of exposure to ethylene include fatigue and headaches." That does seem to fit, though. One of the teachers was holding his head in the refectory.'

'And Master Chang kept touching his head last night!' said Olivier.

'Plus we've all got headaches,' said Matt. 'And I don't know about the rest of you, but I feel sleepy too.'

'Yeah, me too,' said Catarina.

Shawn nodded, then winced.

'So what are you saying?' said Olivier. 'Someone's trying to knock us out?'

'Someone could be releasing sleeping gas into the air,' said Shawn.

'But since when did sleeping gas smell of cherry blossom?' said Olivier.

'Well, it's a mystery,' said Matt. 'And investigating mysteries –'

'– is our game!' finished Catarina.

'But where do we start?' said Olivier.

'What I think is this,' said Matt. 'It's the teachers that seem to be the worst affected. Now, where were they all last night?'

'In the Assembly Hall,' said Catarina, 'for the meet and greet.'

'Right,' said Matt. 'Then that's where we'll start!'

TIGERS IN TREES

They quickly made their way to the Assembly Hall, riding on the moving pavement. The corridors were beginning to fill with people, students chatting excitedly about the tournament, and a few teachers looking decidedly unwell. Nearly everyone was stepping on to the strip of pavement that travelled in the opposite direction to the one the Tangshan Tigers were going in. The tournament was to take place in the *dojo*, as they called the martial arts hall in Japan, on the other side of the school.

One of the Kyoto team, Martina, spotted them and called out. 'Hey, where are you guys going? You should be going the other way!'

'It's OK,' said Olivier quickly. 'We're just sorting something out for Master Chang – we'll see you over at the *dojo*!'

Before Martina could ask any more questions, the moving pavements had carried them too far apart to continue the conversation.

They stepped off near the Assembly Hall and walked along the wide corridor that led to it. There was no one around on this side of the building. The Assembly Hall was a grand bowl-shaped auditorium with high, glass double doors. They stood outside, looking in.

'Nice,' said Olivier appreciatively. 'See the

picture of the fox over the doors? That's a symbol of Kyoto; there's a fox-shrine here.'

'Yeah, well, we're dealing with someone who's cunning like a fox,' said Matt. 'But we're going to focus like eagles – remember what Chang said? Now, let's think. The question is: if someone put sleeping gas in there – assuming that's what happened – how would they do it?'

Shawn looked up and around at the walls and ceiling outside the hall.

'They obviously didn't carry gas canisters in themselves,' he said. 'Otherwise they'd have been affected by it too. And if they'd pumped the gas in through the door or windows, they'd have been seen. It must have been through the air-con system – it's the only possibility.'

He pointed up at an air vent near the ceiling. 'That looks like it might lead through to the hall.'

'Let's see then!' said Catarina.

She went to the wall and put her foot on the central heating unit there, standing up and reaching for the window sill above. She pulled herself up, and now she was halfway to the air vent. Matt watched in admiration as she found a tiny crack in the wall to get her fingers into, a minute bulge in the plaster for a toe-hold, and climbed her way up. He was amazed by her agility. It was like watching a lizard climb up a pane of glass.

She reached the air vent and looked through. 'Yeah, it leads to the hall,' she said. 'I can see the auditorium. And it's pretty wide. I'd say you could get tons of gas through there.'

She climbed down as nimbly as she'd ascended.

'But how did they get up there?' asked Shawn. 'Not everyone can climb like Catarina!'

73

'Anyone could use a ladder, though,' said Olivier. 'And if all the teachers were in the hall no one would see.'

Matt began to feel worried. 'Chang must have breathed in a lot of that stuff,' he said. 'How long's he going to be affected by it? Do you think he'll be OK?'

'It must have been a pretty low dose or he wouldn't still be walking around,' said Shawn, 'and nor would the others. It'll be out of his system soon, I'd say, and he'll be back to normal.'

'But who would do a thing like that?' asked Olivier. 'What's the point of it?'

'Some sort of experiment?' said Matt. 'Or maybe it was a trial run – but what for?'

'Some people are sick!' said Catarina.

'What should we do?' asked Shawn. 'Do you reckon we should tell Chang?'

'We have no hard evidence,' Olivier

pointed out. 'All we've proved is it's possible someone's been squirting sleeping gas around.'

'I don't think Chang is in a state to deal with it right now, anyway,' said Matt. 'We'll have to solve this by ourselves. Let's think: if you wanted to get hold of sleeping gas in a school, where's the best place to look?'

'The science labs!' said Shawn.

'Right,' said Catarina. 'So we should head over to the science department next to look for clues.'

'Only trouble is,' said Matt, 'the science lab is on the same side as the *dojo*.' There was a plan of the school in the atrium and Matt had memorized it when they'd arrived. 'There're gonna be loads of people over there and we'd be spotted for sure!'

They didn't have much time – the tournament was scheduled to begin at eleven o'clock, an hour and a half from now.

'I've got it,' said Matt. 'Those cherry trees all around the school – they don't just smell nice, they'd make great camouflage!'

'What do you mean?' demanded Catarina. 'We should cover ourselves in petals and –'

'No!' said Matt. 'I mean, if we climbed up in them. They're so close together you could easily make your way from one to the next. That way, we could skirt right round the school and get to the science lab from outside.'

'Oh yeah!' said Catarina, punching the air with her fist. This was just the sort of challenge she enjoyed. Anything to do with climbing and she was in her element.

'Let's go,' said Olivier.

They scrambled through an open window into the grounds. The cool fresh air and scent of blossom hit Matt immediately. His head felt clearer now. Much clearer.

'Which way, Matt?'

'That way,' said Matt, pointing. 'Down to the end and round the back.'

Catarina hoisted herself up into the nearest tree as though this was something she did every day. A shower of petals fell, but once up among the branches she was almost completely shielded from view.

Shawn went next, then Olivier.

Matt looked up at the tree. He had never had a great head for heights and the whole journey would have to happen several metres above ground. *Focus*, he told himself. *Put the fear of falling out of your mind; ignore it, just like you ignored the snakes.* The image of the still, peaceful rock garden came into his mind and he felt calmer. He took a deep breath and climbed up.

It was tricky, climbing from one tree to the next. Matt felt the petals tickling his nose and obscuring his vision. And the cherry trees had slender branches that bent under his weight. Several times Matt had to move quickly before the branch gave way beneath him.

He came to a place where there was a wider than usual gap between one tree and the next. He couldn't reach across. He stopped. He felt the branch he was on bending underneath him. If he fell from here it was quite a drop. What was he going to do? He felt a tingling of dread in his stomach.

'You can do it, Matt!' called Catarina. She was three trees ahead of him. 'Jump to the next tree. You can't miss it!'

Matt took a deep breath. He braced his feet against the branch he was on and launched himself. There was nothing but empty space between him and the ground.

Then he hit the next tree, felt the rough bark against his hands, and held on. He breathed out. He'd made it!

'Thanks, Catarina,' he called out shakily.

'Hey, no problem.'

After that, he made steadier progress. About two-thirds of the way along, Matt looked up to see that Catarina had come to a stop. Shawn and Olivier halted too.

'What's up?' called Matt.

'Look,' said Catarina. Her pointing finger emerged from a cloud of pink petals. Matt looked and saw that they were just about level with one of the bedrooms. The curtains were open and through the window he saw Chang sitting on the bed, his head in his hands.

The head teacher of the Kyoto Institute, Mr Ito, was standing with him, talking and looking serious. He was clearly agitated about something – he was gesticulating urgently, as if trying to persuade Chang of something. Matt saw him point in the direction of the *dojo*. Chang raised his head from his hands and said something. Mr Ito didn't answer at once. He looked as though he didn't like what Chang said, but couldn't argue with it. He slowly, reluctantly, nodded. Matt wished he could hear what they were saying.

At that moment Chang turned and looked out of the window. He was staring straight at the tree where Matt was concealed. Matt froze. Could Chang see him?

There was a long, still moment. Then Chang rose from the bed and walked out of the room, accompanied by Mr Ito.

Matt was in no doubt now that there was something serious going on. And Chang and Mr Ito seemed to have some inkling of it. They would have to get to the science lab and solve the mystery before anything else happened. If the sleeping gas saboteurs had struck once, they could strike again.

'OK, let's get moving,' he said. Catarina swung herself into the next tree, and they resumed their progress with greater urgency.

They reached the back of the building and dropped down neatly from the trees, brushing petals from their clothes.

Matt tried the nearest door. It opened. 'The science lab is on the second floor,' he said. 'Come on!'

There was no one around. They hurried up the stairs and came to a door that said SCIENCE DEPARTMENT in English, beneath what Matt guessed were Japanese characters, and then in about ten other languages below that. In smaller letters underneath was the name of the head of the faculty, Mr Burgess, both in English and in *katakana*, the Japanese script used for foreign names.

'Someone should stand guard,' said Olivier. 'We're not supposed to be here – we don't want to get caught now we've got this far.'

'OK,' said Matt. 'You and Catarina stay here and keep a lookout. Shawn and I will go in. If anyone comes, start singing!'

'Singing what?'

'It doesn't matter!' said Matt.

The science department was one large, modern, extremely hi-tech laboratory with gleaming polished plastic surfaces, and windows all the way round.

'We'd better stay low,' said Matt. 'We're visible through these windows from every side.'

He and Shawn went down on all fours and crawled behind the work-benches.

'Where would they keep the sleeping gas stuff?' wondered Matt aloud.

'In the supply cabinet, I'd guess.'

Matt saw a cabinet with steel doors in an alcove at the end of the room. They were safe from view here. They stood up and Matt tried the door.

Locked.

Of course it's locked! thought Matt. No one would leave a cabinet full of dangerous chemicals open. They'd come so far and now they were thwarted. There was no way they were going to get those steel doors open with their bare hands.

But Shawn was reaching nonchalantly into his pocket. He drew out a small silver instrument, shaped a bit like a water pistol with a rubber nozzle at the end.

'What's that?'

'Something my uncle sent me – he's an inventor, you know? It's a universal key. Look, it's filled with water, see, and there's a sealed chamber of liquid nitrogen inside. You just push the rubber bit into the lock, like this, then you press the button, like this, and that breaks the seal. The nitrogen freezes the water instantly, and it forms into the shape of the inside of the lock – so you've got an ice key, see? And the beautiful bit is that the ice then melts and there's no sign of how you got in! Pretty neat, huh?'

'It's brilliant!' said Matt. 'Let's see if it works.'

'Course it works!'

Shawn inserted the rubber part into the lock. He pressed the button. There was a hiss as the nitrogen was released. Then he turned the universal key and the steel door clicked and swung open.

Facing them was a refrigerated storage cabinet with an array of bottles ranged upon shelves, filled with liquids, some clear, some yellow, some green, some purple. Below each bottle was a neat label: *Potassium, Mercury, Sulphuric Acid, Sodium, Copper Sulphate* . . .

And there was one empty space, plain as a missing tooth.

The label on the shelf beneath it said C_2H_4 *Ethylene*.

Matt breathed a long slow breath. 'That's it. Someone has been spraying sleeping gas around!'

'But I still don't understand,' said Shawn. 'It's supposed to smell sweet, but not of cherry blossom.'

'I don't understand either. But let's look around while we're here – see what else we can find.'

Matt closed the supply cabinet and the steel doors re-locked with a click. He turned to a wall cupboard nearby with its door slightly ajar. He threw it wide open. Inside was a higgledy-piggledy jumble of science equipment – Bunsen burners, retort stands, flasks and Petri dishes.

And a bottle with pink mush at the bottom.

Matt picked it up, uncorked the stopper and sniffed. The scent of cherry blossom flooded his nostrils, almost making him cough. He handed it to Shawn.

'Here – smell that.'

'Someone's been extracting essence of cherry blossom!'

'But why?'

Shawn smacked his forehead. 'Why didn't I think of it before?' he exclaimed. 'The smell of cherry blossom was there to disguise the smell of the ethylene! They've mixed the two together, do you see? An unusual sweet smell might make people suspicious – but everyone's used to smelling cherry blossom at this time of year in Kyoto!'

'You're right!' said Matt. 'It's obviously an inside job then – someone at the school. But who? One of the students? Or the science teacher, Mr Burgess?'

'But why would he want to put people to sleep?'

'Why would anyone want to?'

Suddenly they heard a burst of song from outside. Two songs, in fact – it sounded as though Catarina was singing 'The Yellow Rose of Texas' while Olivier was singing 'Old MacDonald Had a Farm'.

Matt and Shawn looked at each other, momentarily paralyzed.

Then the door handle began to turn.

Someone was coming in.

TRICKY DECISIONS

Matt and Shawn dived down behind the teacher's desk.

On all fours, Matt peered through the legs of the table. A student walked in and Matt recognized him at once. It was the tall boy with the cropped blond hair, the one who'd glared at the martial arts teams with such hostility at supper last night. What was he doing here?

The boy marched to the supply cabinet and opened it with a key. Then he placed a bottle in the empty space and shut the door again. He must have replaced the bottle of ethylene, Matt realized.

He turned on his heel to leave – then stopped. Matt saw that the wide-open door of the cupboard had caught his eye. *Oh, you idiot!* he thought to himself. *Why didn't you shut the door after you?* He glanced at Shawn and they exchanged a grimace.

The boy looked around furtively, but didn't see Matt and Shawn crouched behind the desk.

He took the bottle of cherry blossom essence from the cupboard and carried it over to the sink. He directed a stream of water from the tap into the bottle, shaking it vigorously, then emptied it down the drain. He rinsed the bottle several times and left the tap running so that the last drops of the essence disappeared down the plughole. Then he turned off the tap, replaced the now empty bottle in the equipment cupboard, and left the room.

No! thought Matt. Just a few seconds after they'd made their discovery, all the evidence for it had been destroyed.

He and Shawn crawled out from behind the desk.

'So now we've got no proof!' said Matt.

'At least we know what the guy looks like,' said Shawn. 'We must be able to nail him somehow.'

'We'd better get a move on,' said Matt. 'Let's go tell the others.'

'We were so worried he would catch you – but we couldn't stop him,' said Catarina. 'He started to question us, asking what we were doing here.'

'What did you say?' asked Matt.

Olivier grinned. 'Oh, I spun him a line about how we were looking for Mr Burgess, because we'd heard what a brilliant scientist he was and we wanted to get his autograph.'

They all laughed.

'We haven't got much time to waste,' said Matt. 'We must get after that boy, fast!'

'Why, what was he doing in the lab?'

Matt and Shawn quickly explained.

'Yeah, you're right – sounds like he is the one who made the sleeping gas, for sure,' said Catarina, nodding.

'And he may do it again,' said Olivier.

'He may already have done it!' said Shawn suddenly. 'He replaced the ethylene bottle just now – that could mean he's been using it this morning. And if the sleeping gas attack last night was a try-out, this could be the real biggie!'

'But why?' said Olivier. 'Why's he doing it?'

'We won't know till we find him,' said Matt. 'So let's go!'

'Right!' said the Tangshan Tigers, each of them setting off down the corridor at a run.

They pelted through the maze of passages, up and down stairs. No sign of the blond boy. At the foot of a flight of stairs, however, they ran into Miguel, who had already changed into his martial arts suit.

'Where are you guys going? You look like you're in a hurry – but you're going the wrong way for the tournament! Are you lost?'

'No,' said Matt. 'We – we're looking for someone.'

'Who?'

'A tall blond boy – very short hair – do you know him?'

'Why are you looking for him?'

'Er, well –' said Matt. He liked Miguel, but

he didn't feel he knew him well enough to confide their suspicions. After all, the boy was a schoolmate of Miguel's – he might even be a friend of his. They couldn't start making accusations before they had any proof. 'We're looking for him because, er . . .'

'To give him his watch back,' cut in Olivier smoothly. 'We saw him come out of the science lab – we've just been having a look-round the school, you know – and when we went into the lab his watch was there, on the side by the sink.'

'And here's the watch,' said Shawn, producing one from his pocket. Shawn always had a hi-tech gadget or two about his person. Today he had a watch that told the time in five different time zones, with a compass and a stopwatch function.

Miguel looked at it and whistled. 'That's a nice piece of work. Sort of thing that might belong to Andrei Drago. He's a tall blond kid, and if he left it up in the science lab, that figures. He's mad about science.'

'That must be it then,' said Matt. 'Andrei Drago. So, he's mad about science, is he?'

'Yeah, he's a bit of a whizz-kid. His dad's a famous European scientist – Russian, I think. That's all Andrei's interested in – well, that and martial arts. Look over here.'

Miguel took them over to a trophy cabinet mounted on the wall. There was a silver scroll saying *Kyoto Science Prize*, inscribed with Andrei Drago's name three times. On another shelf was the silver cup the martial arts team had won when they'd beaten Tokyo. This was inscribed with all the team members' names, and Matt saw the name of Andrei Drago.

'So, he's in your martial arts team?' said Catarina.

'He used to be,' said Miguel. 'And he was pretty good too. But then your old team-mate, Dani, came along and was even better, so Andrei was dropped.'

It hadn't occurred to Matt to consider this before. At the Beijing end, Dani's leaving had been good news for the reserve, a boy called Jahmal, who'd moved up into the squad to take his place. But it must have been bad news at the Kyoto end for the boy who was dropped to make way for Dani.

'How did he take it?' asked Matt.

'Well, he was pretty sore about it. He's normally a quiet kid, but he did kick up a fuss. You can understand it, I guess. He seems to have got over it now, though.'

The Tangshan Tigers looked at each other. They were all thinking the same thought: Andrei Drago hadn't exactly got over it. Not unless putting the whole Academy to sleep was his way of 'getting over' things.

'Well, thanks,' said Matt. 'We'll see if we can find him.'

'Better be quick,' said Miguel. 'The tournament starts in half an hour — and you guys aren't even changed!'

'Don't worry,' said Catarina. 'We'll be there!'

'See you later then.' Miguel started to walk away, then stopped and turned. 'Hey — and good luck!'

'You too!' said Matt.

'What do you think?' said Catarina. 'Do we carry on looking? Or leave it until after the tournament?'

'We've got thirty minutes,' said Matt. 'Let's find him, if we can. I know Chang's taught us to focus and ignore all distractions but — well, this is quite a distraction!'

'OK, so let's keep looking,' said Shawn.

They began to run towards a side door that led out to the grounds – but the figure of Chang Sifu unexpectedly appeared round the corner.

'Ah,' he said quietly. 'Tangshan Tigers. Your team is worried about you – tournament begins shortly.'

'How are you, sir?' asked Matt. 'Are you feeling –' He stopped, not quite sure how to go on. Was it rude to draw attention to Chang's strange behaviour?

'I am well,' said Chang. 'Please do not worry about me. Focus instead on what you have to do.'

'On the tournament,' said Catarina.

'On the tournament and – whatever other business you have to attend to. But hurry. You have not much time. You must get back to *dojo*.' He handed Catarina a piece of paper. 'Here is team sheet. Go!'

97

Matt and the Tigers ran back to the moving pavement that took them in the direction of the *dojo*. They were just getting off at the other end when they heard a shout.

'Hey! What have you guys been doing?'

It was Carl Warrick – and with him were Abdul, Lola, Wolfgang, Jahmal and the rest of the Beijing squad, running towards them, all dressed in their martial arts suits.

'We need to go and get ready for the tournament,' said Wolfgang. 'They're waiting for us. Chang came to look for you.'

'We know,' said Catarina. 'I've got the team sheet here.'

'But where have you lot been?' said Carl angrily. 'The contest starts in twenty minutes – you can't run out on us like this!'

'We weren't running out on you –' began Catarina.

'Fine captain you turned out to be!' said Carl. 'Wandering off just before the tournament begins.'

'Carl, as your team captain, I say one thing to you, OK? Give your mouth a rest.'

Carl opened his mouth, then closed it again. He went red with anger.

Catarina turned to the Tangshan Tigers. 'It looks like we have to go. Come on, we'll talk about the – the other thing later.'

There didn't seem to be any choice. With an uneasy feeling in the pit of his stomach, Matt followed the others through the corridor to the *dojo* and changing rooms.

Catarina addressed the team. 'OK, guys – I got the team sheet here, showing who's fighting who.' She stuck the sheet to the wall and the squad crowded round. Matt saw that he was down to fight Dani, and his heart sank slightly. That was something he could definitely have done without.

'The main thing is,' went on Catarina, 'you all know that we can win this, if we fight to our best ability. And to do that we must focus, like Master Chang said. So I say we spend these few minutes just focusing, thinking about our fight, how we're going to approach it, clearing our minds of everything else, OK? Everyone close their eyes, sit still and just focus.'

Matt closed his eyes. He slowed his breathing. He tried to think calmly about what to do. There were only a few minutes to go – but was there any way of tackling Andrei Drago before the tournament began? He needed to talk to the other Tigers in private. But how? An idea came to him.

Matt let a minute go by, then he gently nudged Catarina. She opened her eyes. Matt made a chopping motion with his hand. 'Focusing time over,' he mouthed.

'OK, guys,' said Catarina. 'You can open your eyes now.'

'How about the rest of the team go out in the *dojo* now and start to warm up?' suggested Matt. 'We still need to get changed, but the others –'

'Good call, Matt,' said Catarina. 'Get out there, team, and do your warm–up exercises, and we'll join you in a minute.'

'But why can't we all go out together?' objected Carl.

'Because I'm the captain,' said Catarina pleasantly, 'and you do what I say.'

The team filed out.

'Now,' said Matt, 'let's think. Is there anything we can do about Andrei in the next five minutes?'

'I reckon we'd better!' said Shawn. ''Cause

I just thought of something that's not too great.'

'What?' said Catarina.

'Andrei's sore at being left out of the Kyoto Squad. Where do you think he's gonna launch the next attack?'

'At the tournament?' said Olivier.

'Definitely! It'll be his revenge. It's just as easy to put the stuff in the air-con system here as it was in the Assembly Hall, isn't it? And he's got everyone right where he wants them.'

It sounded horribly plausible to Matt. The changing rooms were fitted with small high windows that overlooked the *dojo*. Matt stood on a bench and looked down. The *dojo* was filling up with people – there were seats arranged in rows all around the combat area. He saw Chang Sifu sitting beside the Kyoto coach, Sensei Simon, and behind them Mr

Figgis sitting next to Mr Ito. No one seemed to be suffering any ill-effects as yet, and there was no telltale scent of cherry blossom. But then, Andrei Drago would probably have timed it so that the effects began to kick in once the tournament began. That must have been the point of the rehearsal last night, releasing the gas into the Assembly Hall – so that he could calculate the timing accurately.

Matt looked up at the air vent – a silver grille just below ceiling level. It was a long way up, but –

'OK, I'll help you,' said Catarina quietly, following his gaze.

'Help me do what?'

'Climb up to the air vent and crawl along the – what's it called? The tunnel thing?'

'The duct,' said Shawn.

'If Shawn and Olivier give us a leg up,

we'll crawl along the duct then. Till we find this ethylene stuff.'

They'd have to work fast, Matt realized. And the chances were they wouldn't get back in time for the tournament – which meant all four of their matches would be lost by default. It was almost certainly asking too much of the Beijing Academy team to win with a four-match handicap. They were condemning their team to defeat, and Matt hated to do it. But some things were more important than winning a martial arts tournament.

Like not letting a hall full of people get knocked out by an invisible cloud of ethylene gas, for instance.

'How are we going to get that grille off?' asked Olivier.

'With this!' said Shawn. Delving into the pocket of his jacket, which hung on one of the pegs, he brought out another of his gadgets: an electronic screwdriver.

Catarina climbed nimbly on to Olivier's shoulders. Shawn handed her the screwdriver. She stood, balancing expertly on Olivier's shoulders, and reached up to unscrew the screws. There was a low whirring noise and the first screw tumbled out and clattered on the floor. Then the next, and the next. The grille slid out of position, hanging by the final screw. Catarina unscrewed the last screw and the grille fell down, neatly caught by Shawn.

Catarina reached up and hoisted herself into the black hole. She looked down at Matt and nodded. Then she pulled herself right into the duct, and the last Matt saw of her was the soles of her feet.

It was his turn. More climbing – he was getting pretty used to it by now. He clambered on to Shawn's shoulders and, remembering the way Catarina had done it, pulled himself up into the duct.

He found himself in a dark square tunnel, with metal floor and walls. It wasn't much wider than the width of his shoulders. It was nearly but not quite pitch-black – there were enough chinks in the walls to let in gleams of light along the way. He dimly made out the form of Catarina ahead of him.

A final thought struck him. He twisted his head round and called down to Shawn and Olivier.

'Hey, you guys, now we're in, you'd better get out to the *dojo*. Go and fight in the tournament; we're only two down – you could still help win it for us!'

'Right,' said Shawn. 'I hate to leave you but – I guess you're right.'

'Good luck!' said Olivier.

'You too,' said Matt. He hoped that with two Tangshan Tigers in the team, the Beijing Academy could win the tournament. He couldn't help feeling guilty about not being with the team – but saving innocent people from being given a big dose of headache was more pressing. He just hoped they could pull it off in time.

'Are you ready?' he heard Catarina's voice ahead of him in the dark.

'Yeah,' said Matt. 'Let's do it!'

TIME RUNNING OUT

In the distance Matt could hear the electrical
hum of the air-conditioning unit. He felt the
refrigerated air blowing towards him, and
shivered. He kept crawling, but the darkness
and narrowness of the tunnel were beginning
to get to him. There was no way he could
have turned round; there wasn't room. When
it came to getting out again, they'd have to
crawl backwards.

*How much further until we reach the source of
the sleeping gas?* he wondered. And would they

even see it when they came to it? What if
they missed it in the dark?

What if there are rats up here? he thought.
Fear gripped his guts at the idea of being
attacked by evil sharp-toothed little animals
in this dark confined space. He felt his
breathing getting more laboured.

'Are you all right, Catarina?' he called out
softly, to distract himself.

'Not bad, I guess,' her voice came from up
ahead. 'Not great either. I don't like the cold
and dark.'

'We've just got to focus,' said Matt,
remembering Chang's training.

'You're right; we must focus.' Matt thought
he could hear relief in Catarina's voice.

Focus. Like an eagle. That meant
concentrating on the task, not thinking
beyond it. His breathing calmed down. The
image of the still silent garden in the

Buddhist temple came into his head and he held on to it.

A voice crackled into life. It was an announcement from the public address system in the hall below. Matt stopped crawling and listened hard. He could just make out the words above the hum of the air-con unit.

'Attention: could the two members of the Beijing Academy Martial Arts Squad who have not yet checked in report to the *dojo* immediately. You have five minutes before the tournament begins. If the complete squad is not present, the Beijing Academy will forfeit the match. I repeat: you have five minutes to report or Beijing will forfeit the match.'

So they didn't even have the slim chance of winning with two members down, thought Matt. They had no chance at all if he and Catarina couldn't get back in time. It was pretty sickening. Would the other team members blame them? *Possibly – but what choice do we have?* thought Matt.

The hum of the air-con unit was getting louder. Now it was very loud, filling the tunnel – and, for the first time, Matt caught the unmistakable whiff of cherry blossom.

Catarina said two words. 'Hold breath!' She didn't speak again.

Matt sucked in a great lungful of air and shut his mouth. The air wasn't entirely pure but it was only going to get worse from here on in. He forced himself to crawl on, focusing solely on the movement of his limbs.

Ahead of him, Catarina stopped. Matt came up beside her. The duct had widened into a sort of crossroads, with other ducts leading off in different directions. In the centre was the air-conditioning unit, a large black box with a motor throbbing inside and steel grilles on each face.

Taped to the grilles was a large piece of pale cotton gauze, glimmering in the darkness – the kind of surgical gauze that is used for dressing wounds.

Matt and Catarina exchanged silent glances. This had to be it!

Matt reached out and touched the gauze; it was wet, sodden. Andrei must have doused it in the ethylene solution and, as the air blew through it, the solution evaporated into a gas and was blown along the air ducts. It was clever, Matt had to admit.

There was no time to lose. He couldn't hold his breath much longer – and if he breathed in here, this close to the ethylene solution in its strongest concentration, he would pass out. And then he would continue to breathe it in as he lay unconscious . . .

He grabbed a corner of the gauze and pulled. After a moment, it came away with a tearing sound as the tape holding it in place gave way. Matt bundled it into a ball and shoved it inside his martial arts jacket.

Catarina gave him a thumbs-up sign and pointed back the way they had come. Fortunately in this part of the tunnel there was enough space to turn. Catarina set off again on hands and knees: Matt followed as fast as he could, the pain and pressure in his lungs building. Cautiously, he began to breathe out, very, very slowly – what he really needed was to take more air in, but at least expelling the air already inhaled brought some relief of the pressure.

The tunnel seemed endless. Pain grew in his chest. *What a choice*, Matt thought: *either suffocate from not breathing, or breathe in and be knocked out!*

Focus, Matt told himself. *Keep moving, breathe out slowly, don't breathe in . . .*

Just when he thought his lungs would burst, he saw Catarina swing herself down into the hole by which they'd entered.

With only her head and shoulders visible, she said: 'Throw it to me!'

Matt took the rolled-up sodden gauze from his tunic and hurled it at her. She caught it neatly and dropped it down into the changing room.

Matt opened his mouth and drew in great gasps of sweet cold air. It felt wonderful – as if he'd just been saved from drowning.

He turned and lowered his legs through the air vent into the changing room. Catarina grabbed him by the waist to help him with the jump down.

He landed, staggered, regained his balance.

'Thanks, Catarina.'

He wondered if he looked the same as she did: dishevelled, red-faced, exhausted.

The public address system crackled into life again.

'This is the last reminder for the Beijing Academy Team. If the entire team is not present in the *dojo* within one minute, the match will be forfeit. I repeat, the match will be forfeit if the missing squad members do not report within one minute.'

Matt grabbed the saturated gauze and flung it into a locker. It should be safe there until after the tournament – and would provide vital evidence of the attempted sabotage of the tournament.

'Right,' he said, 'let's get down to the *dojo*!'

He and Catarina ran through the changing-room doors and along the passage that led to the stairs.

Catarina didn't bother with the stairs. She

swung one leg over the banister, sat astride it and slid all the way down. *Pretty good tactic,* thought Matt. He flung a leg over the metal banister and pushed off.

They burst into the auditorium just as the electronic clock on the wall was clicking over to 11.00.

THE TOURNAMENT

There was a cheer from the crowd. And a mighty cheer from their own team – apart from Carl.

'We knew you'd make it!' said Shawn.

Olivier looked at Matt questioningly. Matt gave a discreet thumbs-up sign, and saw Olivier's and Shawn's faces relax in relief.

Mr Figgis, in his seat across the hall, was clapping. Chang nodded almost imperceptibly, as though this was entirely what he had expected. He turned and said a few words to Mr Ito, who was sitting behind him.

Carl continued to scowl at them and muttered darkly: 'If you'd cost us the match, you two would have been sorry, I can tell you that!'

'Well, that did not happen, so there is no point thinking about it,' Catarina told him.

There was a hush as Sensei Simon stood up and spoke into the microphone at the judges' table.

'We are very pleased that our guest team made it to the tournament in time – you had us worried for a moment there! Ladies and gentlemen, the tournament will be the best of eleven bouts – the first team to record six victories will be the winner. As you know this is a mixed tournament where various fighting styles are permitted – karate, judo, kung fu, tae kwon-do, capoeira, ju-jitsu

– but the scoring system is simple. A strike, by hand or foot, which makes good contact, scores a point. Only recognized techniques in one of the martial arts disciplines will be counted; wild or accidental contact scores no points. The head is out of the target area. Any fall scores a point, and so does any hold that is unbroken for ten seconds. Each bout is the best of five points. The judges' decision is final.' He indicated the three judges, two men and one woman, sitting behind him. 'The scoring of a point will be recorded thus.' One of the judges pressed a button on the table in front of him: a klaxon sounded and the electronic scoreboard on the wall behind flashed up 1–0. The judge then reset the scoreboard to read 0–0 again.

'The first contest,' said Sensei Simon, 'will be between Dani Valerio of Kyoto, and Matt James of Beijing.'

Matt stood up. He was out of breath, exhausted and his head was aching badly. He must have breathed in more of the gas than he had thought.

He was going to have to focus like he'd never focused before. Like an eagle gliding a mile high, oblivious to everything but a flash of movement on the ground.

Matt walked slowly out to the centre of the arena. He would rather not have been pitted against Dani. He liked him and wasn't sure if he would be able to fight with full aggression. It would have been much easier to fight a stranger. But he had no choice in the matter. He'd have to forget that it was Dani and think of him as an opponent.

Dani approached from the opposite corner. They faced each other. Dani gave a small smile, which Matt did his best to return. They bowed to each other. When they straightened up, Dani's smile had gone. His face wore a set, determined expression. The message was clear: they were friends, but friendship would be forgotten as soon as the bout began. Dani would do his level best to win.

And so will I, thought Matt. But was he capable of his best today? He knew he wasn't on top form; he was tired, his head ached and he felt slightly dizzy. The ethylene he'd breathed in must have affected his balance.

Sensei Simon raised his arm, then let it fall in a chopping motion. It was the signal for the fight to start.

Matt immediately adopted a defensive stance, side-on to Dani, hands ready to block. It would be best to play himself in gradually, not go rushing to the attack. Dani took this as an invitation, going forward and launching a high kick at Matt, which Matt only just managed to block, double-handed – but Dani was already following in with another kick, and this one got in beneath Matt's guard and smacked him firmly in the ribs.

The klaxon sounded. The Kyoto supporters cheered. 1–0 to Dani.

For one horrible moment Matt thought he was going to vomit. He controlled himself with an effort, taking a deep breath.

Sensei Simon signalled for the fight to resume. Dani was coming at him again. It was all one-way traffic – Matt could do nothing but hang in there, blocking Dani's attacks as best he could, giving ground all the time. He knew he ought to counter-attack, hit back with knife-hand thrusts or flying kicks, the sort of dynamic strikes that he specialized in as a tae kwon-do practitioner, but his body didn't feel capable of it. He tried a side-kick, but he made the move half-heartedly and Dani dodged it easily –

worse, he had left himself open and Dani landed a karate chop on his shoulder that made him stagger.

The klaxon blared again. More cheers. 2–0 to Dani.

'C'mon, Matt – focus!' called Catarina.

Yes, that was it. Focus. He needed to empty his mind of everything but this fight, forget how tired he felt, forget his dizziness, forget his aching head.

Focus.

Matt felt something change within him. That image of the rock garden, so still and calm, rose up before him again. His whole mindset was stronger, calmer. He still kept his defensive stance, but it felt different now. *I'm not gonna just soak up attacks any more*, he thought. *I'm gonna go for it, look for a chance to hit back. And hard.*

Dani came in with a flurry of low kicks,

trying to sweep his legs away; Matt blocked with his feet and then, as Dani aimed a punch at him, grabbed the outstretched arm and turned his body into Dani's, forcing Dani round and getting him in an armlock. It was not a classic tae kwon-do move, but one borrowed from ju-jitsu, and it took Dani completely by surprise. He struggled and twisted and tried to counter-punch, but Matt held firm – he counted ten seconds in his head – then he heard the welcome sound of the klaxon blaring.

2–1.

The Beijing Academy team cheered wildly.

'Yeah! Come on, Matt!' shouted Catarina.

It was as if a spring inside him had been released. All his sluggishness had gone. He leapt to the attack. There was a fast exchange of strikes and blocks, but Matt came off best – a knife-hand strike to Dani's midriff sent him reeling, and the klaxon sounded once again.

2–2.

Matt came forward like a greyhound released from its trap as the bout resumed. He feinted a straight-arm punch, forcing Dani to make the block, then launched into a spectacular thrusting front kick, the kick of his life, which took Dani squarely in the sternum and knocked him clean off his feet on to his back.

The klaxon blared, the Beijing team went crazy, the electronic scoreboard flashed up the wonderful score of 2–3!

Dani got to his feet. They bowed to each other.

Matt felt shattered but exhilarated.

Dani gave a rueful smile. 'Well done, Matt. You were too good for me today.'

'Well done to you too. It was a great fight – you made me work for it!'

Matt went back to his team, who applauded him all the way with cheers and whoops.

'That was brilliant, Matt!'

'Well done, Matt!'

'Way to go!'

'Fantastic, Matt!' said Catarina, clapping him on the back. 'You fought so good.'

'Thanks,' said Matt. He was surprised to find that he was trembling.

Stephane was up next, facing a tall mixed-race boy who was a Hung gar kung fu specialist. It was an awkward clash of styles – Stephane, a judo expert, kept trying to get in close to get hold of his opponent and throw him, while the Kyoto fighter was trying to keep Stephane at arm's length so he could pick him off with kicks and punches.

Matt cheered loudly for his team-mate. Stephane fought hard, and did succeed once, putting his opponent flat on his back with a classic ippon-seonage throw – but apart from that, the Kyoto boy was too fast and his reach was too long for Dani to handle comfortably. All too quickly, Dani had taken three hits and the fight was declared in favour of Kyoto.

The tournament was tied at 1–1.

'Bad luck, Stephane,' said Matt sympathetically.

'Win some, lose some,' said Stephane – but Matt could see he was doing his best to conceal his disappointment.

Things went against them in the next two fights too. Vincent lost a close-fought match 3–2; then Lola went down to the same score.

The overall score was: Kyoto Institute of Excellence 3, Beijing International Academy 1.

The Kyoto supporters were shouting

loudly now, confident that victory would be theirs. Another three wins and they would be the champions.

Chang Sifu looked across at his team. He inclined his head ever so slightly. His look seemed to Matt to say: 'Don't give up. You can do it.'

Catarina was up next. Matt touched her arm. 'You OK?'

She still looked tired after their ordeal in the air duct. But she hadn't been in such close contact with the ethylene-soaked gauze as Matt had – plus she'd had longer to recover.

'Sure,' she said. 'I'll be fine.'

'Don't forget – focus!'

'You bet.'

Catarina's opponent was a Chinese girl, short and squat but powerfully built, who moved with deceptive speed. It was odd watching the tall slender Catarina facing her in the arena – like watching a stork facing a bulldog.

Catarina began defensively, trying to stay out of trouble, but it didn't work. The Kyoto girl was a judo expert, but used some ju-jitsu techniques as well. She grabbed Catarina in a neck-hold, keeping it tight for ten seconds and scoring the first point. Shortly afterwards she got in close and put Catarina on the mat with *o-goshi*, or a hip-throw.

Catarina seemed to wake up. Matt knew just how she felt. When he'd been really up against it and staring defeat in the face, he'd remembered to focus. He'd found himself fighting as he knew he could, naturally, in his own style. The same thing was happening with Catarina. She began fighting capoeira-style: dancing, twirling, turning and twisting, throwing punches and high kicks

at unexpected, almost impossible angles.
It was a wonderful display and it brought
the Beijing team to their feet, shouting
her name.

'Go, Catarina!'

'Yes!'

'You can do it, Catarina!'

The Kyoto fighter couldn't cope with the
onslaught; when the klaxon sounded for the
fifth and final time, Catarina was the winner
by three points to two.

Now the Beijing team seemed to be on a
roll. Olivier was the next to fight and won
his bout 3–0 with almost languid ease.

Wolfgang had a tougher time of it, but
managed to prevail over a strong opponent, a
karate fighter, 3–2.

That made it Kyoto 3, Beijing 4.

But not for long. The next Beijing fighter
was Abdul, and he faced a very tough

opponent indeed in a Korean tae kwon-do specialist. Too tough. The Korean won 3–1.

The tournament was tied 4–4.

Now it was Shawn.

'Come on, Shawn!' shouted Matt. 'This match is yours!' All the Beijing team, even Carl, roared their support.

'Go on, Shawn!' shouted Carl. 'Don't let us down!'

Shawn's opponent was a judo expert like himself. They were evenly matched and grappled together for a long time, tugging each other's jackets, attempting to pull the other off balance, sweeping at each other's legs for a long time without either gaining an advantage. At last, Shawn succeeded in lifting the boy off his feet and slamming him down on his back. Then, as soon as the fight resumed, he took his opponent by surprise by attacking with a karate-style kick that

struck the boy on the hip and scored
Shawn's second point. It was a good job,
thought Matt, that Chang had trained them
to be so versatile in their fighting styles:
'Perfect your own style,' he liked to say, 'but
learn other styles too and be flexible enough
to use them.'

But Shawn rashly tried the same move
again. This time the Kyoto fighter was ready
for it; he neatly caught Shawn's foot and
upended him on the mat. And in the next
exchange he came off best too, throwing
Shawn with a simple *o-goshi*.

The match was tied at 2–2, and now Matt
was feeling anxious for his friend. He hoped
Shawn could come back and take the bout,
otherwise they would be one bout away
from overall defeat. *But at least*, he thought,
*no one is dropping down unconscious. At least we
stopped that happening.* Win or lose, it would

be a relief when the tournament was over –
then they could bring the criminal to justice.
He scanned the faces of the audience,
looking for Andrei Drago. Then he saw him,
sitting in the back row on the far side near
an open window, as far away from the
ventilation grille as it was possible to be.
Drago kept glancing round, looking puzzled
and disappointed. *It's not happening, is it?* Matt
thought, suppressing a smile. *Your scheme
didn't work this time, Drago!*

He turned his attention back to Shawn's
bout. The fighters closed for the last time.
Again, there was a tense protracted period
where neither could quite gain an advantage.
Finally the Kyoto fighter stumbled and
Shawn went over with him. Shawn pinned
him to the mat – but the Kyoto fighter kept
struggling and bucking, arching his back. He
couldn't get up, but Shawn couldn't quite

hold him still either. Was the hold good? Matt felt tense as he saw the judges watching closely.

Then the klaxon sounded. Shawn had won 3–2.

A slightly scrappy victory, perhaps, but they all counted, thought Matt. He tousled Shawn's hair as the Beijing fighter returned to the team. 'Nice one.'

'Thanks. It was tough out there,' said Shawn, still breathing hard, but smiling.

5–4 to the Beijing Academy. One more victory and they'd do it!

The next fighter up was Jahmal, the new member of the squad. He fought with great courage and spirit. Unfortunately, his opponent was Miguel, the Kyoto captain, and Miguel was simply too good for him. Miguel won the bout 3–1.

And now it was 5–5 overall and the

atmosphere in the *dojo* had reached boiling point. The Kyoto supporters were shouting their heads off.

'Ky-o-to! Ky-o-to!'

Led by Catarina, the Beijing team did their best to shout against them. Even Mr Figgis lent his voice. 'Bei-jing! Bei-jing!'

But they were so heavily outnumbered they were drowned out by the roar of the home supporters.

Sensei Simon stood up to appeal for calm.

'Please quieten down for the last bout. Allow the fighters to concentrate.' The noise died down, but still simmered at a lower level. The atmosphere was so tense that absolute silence was impossible.

'The final bout will be between Conrad Sienkiewicz and Carl Warrick.'

'Go on, Carl,' said Matt. 'You can do it!'

'I know I can do it,' said Carl. 'Watch and

learn!' He strutted out to the centre of the
arena.

Matt had a good eye for a fighter's
capabilities. He could usually tell, just by
physique, stance and the way a fighter held
him or herself, if they were an opponent to
fear. He could see at a glance that Carl had a
tough task ahead of him. Conrad was a big
tall Polish boy – taller even than Carl, who
was big for his age, and heavier, more
muscular, with broader shoulders. But it
wasn't just his size that impressed Matt; it was
the relaxed way he stood, the light step with
which he walked, the lack of tension in his
body language.

The two fighters bowed to each other, and
then the match was underway.

Carl began explosively, leaping straight into
the attack. This often succeeded against
weaker fighters, whose confidence and

defences crumbled quickly against a direct assault. But the Polish boy was more than equal to it. He was, like Carl, a *karateka* and clearly familiar with the moves. He blocked hard, then hit back and sent Carl crashing to the mat.

1–0 to Kyoto.

When Carl got up he was limping slightly. But eager to make good his loss, he leapt to the attack again, throwing a wild volley of kicks and punches. The Polish boy blocked them all again, then knocked Carl's guard aside to score with a karate chop to the body.

Again the klaxon blared. 2–0 to Kyoto.

Carl had lost his confident air now, Matt saw. He looked tense, desperate, knowing he was only one point away from losing the whole tournament.

'C'mon, Carl,' shouted Catarina. 'Focus!'

137

Matt thought he saw a change in Carl then, as though a new calm and resolve had come to him. The bout resumed. Carl went on with his attacking style – which was wise, thought Matt, as it was the style natural to him – but more purposefully, less wildly. He was carefully testing out the Kyoto fighter's defences. His first few strikes were blocked, but he kept pressing forward until at last he got through the Polish boy's guard and scored with a spear-hand thrust to the body.

2–1! The Beijing team shouted their encouragement.

'Keep focused, Carl!' shouted Catarina.

Carl took her advice. Again he pressed forward, aggressively, persistently. The Polish boy was under real pressure now. He tried to win back the initiative with a roundhouse chest-high kick, but this was a big mistake – Carl neatly swept his other leg from under him and he crashed to the mat just like Carl had done earlier.

2–2!

The noise level had risen again to screaming pitch. But Carl was still focused, Matt saw – his face calm, his eyes determined.

This time it was the Polish boy who leapt to the attack, hoping to finish off quickly a fight that was slipping away from him. Carl blocked his first kick and blocked the follow-up attack, stepping backwards – then unexpectedly stepped into his opponent and hit him with a short-range punch to the midriff. The Polish boy staggered and fell.

The klaxon blared, hardly audible above the din.

3–2 – the Beijing International Academy had won!

Carl came back to the side of the arena,

grinning, to the riotous cheers of his team-mates.

'What did I tell you?' he said to Matt. 'Watch and learn!'

'Nice one, Carl!' said Catarina. 'We did it!'

'I did it, you mean.'

'C'mon, Carl, you fought well, but it was a team effort –' said Catarina.

'All I know is I got you guys out of jail. Without me, we'd be going home without the trophy!'

Matt turned away. There was no point arguing with Carl, and he didn't want to spoil the moment by trying to. Even though the short-range punch that had won Carl the bout was not a karate punch – it was a kung-fu technique he could only have learned from their sifu.

Master Chang was walking over to congratulate them. He was completely back to his normal self, Matt was glad to see — poised, upright, his eyes bright.

'Good work, team!' he said. 'Excellent display of skill, courage — and focus.'

'Sir?' said Matt. 'We've got something to tell you —'

'Something to show you,' said Catarina. 'If you could come to the changing room with us.'

Miguel came over to the Beijing team. 'Congratulations, you guys. We don't like losing at the Kyoto Institute, but I gotta say that was one of the best tournaments ever!'

'We should tell Miguel too,' said Catarina.

'Tell me what?'

'Let's go the changing rooms.'

'Yes,' said Chang Sifu. 'Let us see what you have to show us.'

The Tangshan Tigers led Master Chang and Miguel to the changing rooms.

Matt threw open the locker door. The strong, sweet smell of cherry blossom wafted out.

'Don't breathe too close to that piece of gauze,' said Matt. 'It's soaked in ethylene, disguised with cherry blossom extract. It's been hidden in the air-conditioning system – that's the reason people have been getting headaches. That's the reason you were so sleepy last night, sir.'

Chang gazed at him. Miguel burst out: 'But that's impossible! Who would do a thing like that?'

'Perhaps someone who held a grudge about being dropped from martial arts team would do a thing like that,' said Chang.

'You mean Andrei? But he wouldn't –'

Chang stepped lightly up on to the bench and looked through the window at the *dojo* below. 'Come and see,' he said.

Chapter 8

SEARCHING FOR ANDREI

The Tangshan Tigers and Miguel looked down into the hall. Two uniformed security guards were talking to a sullen-faced Andrei Drago. Suddenly, Drago made a break for it, jumping over the row of chairs in front and racing for the door. The security guards gave chase. Sensei Simon blocked the exit door. Drago doubled back and, desperate to escape, came running towards the changing rooms. *He's coming this way*, Matt realized. Drago disappeared from sight. A moment later and Drago burst into the room.

He stopped at the sight of Chang, Miguel and the Tangshan Tigers. A hunted expression came over his face. He turned to run out again – but Matt and Miguel were too quick. They pounced on him, grabbing an arm each. Drago bucked and struggled, but he couldn't break free.

'Let me go!' he spat.

'Why?' asked Catarina. 'So you can go and drug a few more people?'

'You mind your own business – why did you have to come sticking your noses into my plans?'

'I kind of think it was our business, considering you were trying to sabotage our tournament,' said Matt.

'How could you do a thing like that?' Miguel demanded. 'You're a disgrace to the Kyoto Institute!'

'Oh, you don't understand. None of you understands a thing. You're all morons and I'll be glad to see the back of this place!'

Chang stepped forward and raised his hand. 'Enough,' he said. Matt marvelled at the way his voice, though quiet, carried such authority. Drago immediately fell silent. 'This is not place to discuss this. You must go and answer Ito-san's questions.'

The two uniformed security guards arrived, panting. 'Take him to Ito-san's office, please,' said Chang. 'Inform Ito-san I shall arrive shortly.'

The guards led Drago away.

'So – you mean, you knew all along?' asked Matt, incredulous.

Chang nodded slowly. 'I had suspicions after events of last night. I knew Drago had been dropped from team and what I saw of him made me sure he still held grudge.

Sensei Simon told me about him and I knew he had scientific know-how to make such a plan work.'

'But – why didn't you say anything?' asked Miguel.

'I did. I confided suspicions to Mr Ito. We agreed to watch and wait. You saw me holding this conversation with Ito-san in my room – when you were concealed in cherry trees, you remember.'

The Tangshan Tigers looked at one another. So he had known they were there! Was there anything Chang Sifu did not know?

'We had no evidence to confront Drago,' Chang went on, 'nor, at this time, did we know how he was spreading invisible sleeping gas cloud. Nothing to do but wait for Drago to strike again and get evidence against him. When I saw Matt and Shawn burst into tournament late, and I saw Matt give thumbs-up sign to friends, I knew danger had been averted and that there would now be witnesses, perhaps concrete evidence. I notified Mr Ito and that is why security guards came to take Drago away as soon as tournament ended.'

'But – wasn't it risky to let Drago carry on with it?'

'Risk was unavoidable,' said Chang. 'Besides, perhaps it was not such a great risk – not when the Tangshan Tigers are involved!'

Matt felt a warm glow of pride. Chang had known the Tangshan Tigers would come to the rescue – that was how much he trusted them.

At this point Carl sidled into the changing room, curious to know what was going on.

'Who are the Tangshan Tigers?' asked Miguel, puzzled.

'Ah, one day, if you are very lucky, you

may have the honour to know Tangshan Tigers,' said Chang. 'As for me, I have the honour to call them my friends.'

He turned and walked slowly from the room.

'Hey, he's quite a guy, your coach!' said Miguel.

'Yes,' said Matt, 'he is.'

Carl scowled at the Tangshan Tigers. 'Ooh, "I have the honour to call them my friends",' he said in a mimicking voice. 'What is he on?'

'Don't take any notice,' Catarina said to the others. 'He's just jealous.'

'I am not!' said Carl, and stormed out.

'Sorry about him,' said Matt. He felt vaguely responsible for Carl, as a team-mate. 'He gets a bit funny sometimes.'

'Don't worry about it,' said Miguel. 'Every school has a few like that. I mean, we have Drago!'

'Yeah, that's true,' said Matt. Carl might be a pain, but at least he didn't go around drugging people.

The next day the sun was high in the sky, the scent of cherry blossom was in the air and the team were about to board the coach that would take them back to the airport.

Matt looked around in puzzlement. There was no sign of Chang Sifu.

'Where's Chang?' he asked.

'He told me to tell everyone he will meet us at the airport,' said Mr Figgis. 'He has some business to sort out here first – he's going to come along by taxi.'

'What business?' asked Shawn.

'He will explain all about that to you later, I'm sure.'

Strange, thought Matt – but then that was often the way with Chang. You never quite knew what he was up to, but there always turned out to be a good reason for it.

Miguel and the Kyoto team had come out to wish them goodbye.

'Well done, you guys,' said Miguel. 'Maybe we'll face you again in a return match someday.'

'Hope so,' said Catarina. 'It was great!'

'It certainly wasn't dull!' said Miguel. He held out his hand. 'Goodbye.'

Matt shook his hand warmly. So did the rest of the squad. Then they boarded the coach and waved through the windows as the coach swung out into the traffic.

Matt was looking forward to getting back to Beijing. The Academy felt like home to him now. It had been a fantastic adventure, but it would be fun to be back there, telling everyone all about it.

★

They boarded the jet. There was still no sign of Chang, though, and Matt was beginning to feel anxious.

'Where is he? He'll miss the plane if he doesn't hurry!'

'Don't worry,' said Olivier. 'Chang always –'

He broke off as Chang Sifu appeared in the doorway of the plane. He stood in the centre of the aisle.

'Sorry for delay,' said Chang. 'Before take-off, I have a special announcement. We lost a valuable squad member in Dani, as you know, but I have arranged exchange with Kyoto Institute. We will be getting a new pupil – one of most gifted young scientists studying in Asia. I ask you all to make him welcome!'

Chang stood aside – and Matt's jaw dropped. Behind Chang stood the tall, blond-haired, hard-faced figure of Andrei Drago.

'Hi, I'm looking forward to being on your

team,' said Andrei, as if the incident with the sleeping gas had never happened at all. As if he'd never tussled with security guards.

What on earth was Chang thinking? Matt couldn't get his head round it – to invite the boy behind the sleeping-gas attacks to join the Beijing Academy? It didn't make sense!

'But – that's –' began Catarina. Chang silenced her with a warning glance. He looked at each of the Tangshan Tigers in turn, and his look said, as clearly as if he had spoken: 'Say nothing.'

Matt looked at the other Tigers. They all shrugged helplessly.

Matt sank into his seat and gazed out of the window as the plane took off. The cherry trees were tiny pink dots below them. Beijing was just a few hours away. Matt looked round the head-rest of his seat. Further down the aisle, Andrei was flicking through a martial arts magazine. His lips curved in a thin smile. He put the magazine down and looked up. He raised his eyebrows at Matt insolently. It was a clear challenge. Matt held his gaze steadily. Then Andrei closed his eyes and leaned his head back to sleep.

Matt turned back round.

'What's going on?' whispered Shawn.

Catarina and Olivier looked at Matt anxiously.

'I don't know,' said Matt. He could feel his heart thudding in his chest. 'This must be something pretty big – something important. Chang would have to have a really good reason.'

'But what reason could it be?' demanded Catarina.

'I don't know,' said Matt again. 'But I guess we'll find out.'

Join the Team and Win a Prize!

Do YOU have what it takes to be a Tangshan Tiger?

Answer the questions below for the chance to win an exclusive Tangshan Tigers kit bag. Kit bag contains T-shirt, headband and cloth badge.*

1. What is the Chinese term for 'training hall'?

   a) Kwoon   **b)** Karateka **c)** Kufu

2. Catarina's specialty is capoeira. Which country does this martial art come from?

   a) Britain   **b)** Bolivia   **c)** Brazil

3. In Karate, a sequence of movements performed without a partner is called _kata_.

   a) True   **b)** False

Send your answers in to us with your name, date of birth and address. Each month we will put every correct answer in a draw and pick out one lucky winner.

Tangshan Tigers Competition, Puffin Marketing, 80 Strand, London WC2R 0RL

Closing date is 31 August 2010.

Open to UK residents aged 6 or over. If you are under 13 you will need to include written permission from your parent or guardian

For full terms and conditions visit puffin.co.uk. Promoter is Penguin Books Limited. No purchase necessary

*subject to change